DOWN ON
FRIEN[...]

Fiddlesticks and gumd[...] ...come to "Down on Friendly Acres," a series based on the life of a real family – my family – the Friend family. My parents were farmers. They raised crops, livestock, and me, along with my two brothers and sister, on a farm rightly named Friendly Acres.

I was raised on the farm in the 1950's and 1960's. Things were very different then and even more different when my parents were children. My parents never watched television. Television hadn't been invented yet. My parents listened to the radio, but Grandma Brombaugh, born in 1907, grew up without televisions, radios, or cars. As a farmer's daughter, she learned to drive a horse and buggy and could easily guide a mule and plow.

Born one year earlier in 1906 was Philo Farnsworth, a farmer's son. At fourteen, Philo was plowing a field of potatoes when the lights went off in his head. His vision of how light reflected on the rows later aided him in 1927 to transmit a television image comprised of 60 horizontal lines. That image was a dollar sign. This played a vital role in the invention of the television – which goes to show you just how smart farmers really are.

In 1961, the year this book takes place, Saturday morning cartoons began. Television shows were broadcast on only three stations – ABC, CBS, and NBC.

After the last show each day, the Star Spangled Banner would play to conclude the evening's broadcast. Then the television made a funny noise, a snow storm appeared on the screen, and shows weren't televised again until the next morning.

Patriotism flourished as most families had loved ones that served in the armed forces. They fought for the freedom of religion and speech that we cherish today. My father, Sergeant Harold Friend, was a tank commander in World War II. He received a Bronze Star for his "great courage and devotion to duty" and "making his way for 50 yards under an intense barrage of hostile fire . . . completely disregarded his personal safety by leaving his tank (he rushed) to the aid of two men and an officer."

My father was an American hero. I believe my mother, Jean, was a hero, too. As a child, she left an indelible impression on my life. According to Noah Webster, "indelible" means "cannot be rubbed out or removed." I'll never forget when our neighbor's little girl, Connie, was in an accident. Sowing seeds of a different kind, my mother was filled with compassion and walked alongside her. Mother conveyed love, joy, and hope to Connie by giving her a Sunshine Basket.

As a writer, I have the liberty of intertwining truth with fiction and truth with truth. In this book, the little girl is actually based on the true story of another girl, LeAnne Taylor. LeAnne is a dear friend of mine, and we share much in common. We're farmer's daughters with dark hair and brown eyes, and former 4-H members. We both play the piano and love to talk.

LeAnne has been a television personality for over twenty years. Recently diagnosed with cancer, LeAnne faced her battle with great courage and allowed her audience to walk alongside her. Her family, faith, and friends played a vital role in her recovery. LeAnne is a cancer survivor – a hero in my book, too.

True heroes are real – not make believe. Most heroes, like my father, need not brag about their accomplishments. I encourage you to look around and see who the heroes are in your life. One usually doesn't have to look too far. They're heroes because they never hesitated to treat others better than themselves. My two favorite heroes are my parents. I've written it again and again but it's worth repeating; my parents not only "talked the talk, they walked the walk."

Who's your hero? Take time to tell them why. Grandma Brombaugh always says, "Presents put a smile on a face for a day but kind words bring love, joy, and hope to the heart forever!" Make a habit of planting seeds of kindness.

Again as a writer, I have the liberty of intertwining non-fiction with fiction. Grab your detective gear, visit our website – www.DownOnFriendlyAcres.com – and enter the contest to see if you can discover the flaw in this book with 1961 history!

Let's take a walk down on **Friendly Acres** *and... fiddlesticks and gumdrop bars!!! I've run out of room again. Remember,*

I'M A FRIEND and U R 2!

R. Friend

DEDICATION

...in memory and honor of my mother, Jean Friend, for her overflowing compassion for mankind, her incredible zeal for life, her unconditional sacrifice for her family, her grace and courage shown in facing her own battle with cancer, and her living example – "Sunshine or rain, always and forever, dare to dance, and leap for joy!"

...in honor of my father, Harold Eugene Friend, for being a shining example of a true friend and hero – one who was willing to lay down his life for a friend, for showing his family the importance of hard work but always reminding us that work was never more important than making memorable magical moments with his family, and for his unconditional love and commitment to his family and friends.

...in honor of everyday heroes who cross our paths sharing love, joy, and hope to friends and strangers.

...to my family – the sunshine of my life – who radiates warmth, cheer, and happiness and focuses on the 3 F's – family, faith, and friends...my husband, Bill, for believing in our mission - my children, Jeremy and Stephanie, for setting out on missions of their own.

I love you!!!

R. FRIEND

Hats Off To Heroes

Down On
Friendly Acres
#3

SUNFLOWER SEEDS PRESS

ISBN 9780974362724 Paperback
ISBN 9780974362755 Hardcover

Text copyright © 2005 "R. Friend" Ronda Friend
Illustrations by Bill Ross
Graphic design by Julie Wanca Design
First Printing - Sunflower Seeds Press
All rights reserved. Published by Sunflower Seeds Press, PO Box 1476, Franklin, Tennessee 37065

Library of Congress Control Number 2005931780

Printed in the U.S.A.
First Printing, Second Printing, Third Printing - Sunflower Seeds Press

CONTENTS

The Friend Family

Duane, Ronda, Diane, and Ronald

CHAPTER 1

Feature Creature!

Fiddlesticks and gumdrop bars! Where was Diane? I'd checked under the bed and in the closets. The only things on Diane's bed were bedcovers in a huge wad. My baby sister could have been hidin' anywhere in this old house, but it was *definitely* not in our room. Where was she?

There are more nooks 'n crannies in our house than Babe Ruth's home runs. *Friendly Acres'* farmhouse was built in 1850. It's over one hundred years old. Nooks 'n crannies provide for some spooky places – 'specially if you don't know much about them. However, nooks 'n crannies make great places to play hide-n-seek. Along with countless closets and dozens of doors, this old house has a dark, dingy attic, a laundry chute, a humongous fireplace in the parlor, a dumbwaiter, and an endless cellar.

The scariest nook 'n cranny is the attic. Diane would *never* hide there - neither would I! The only way to the attic is through our bedroom. Three large wooden steps lead up to a huge wood paneled door that creaks when it's opened. The black wrought iron latch keeps the door shut. Behind the door are more steps that curve and wind into total darkness. I've only been up there twice with Daddy. I told him the attic is *spooky!* Daddy laughs and tells me I'm *kooky!*

Kooky? Daddy is quite a joker. When he first called me *kooky,* I didn't like the sound of the word. Ronald, my older brother, *Mr. World Book Worm Encyclopedia* told me that a kook sometimes means a crazy person. But when I spent the night at Grandma Brombaugh's house last month, we looked up *kooky* in the dictionary. According to Noah Webster,

---

koo·ky / ' kü-kE / *adjective*
having the characteristics of a kook

kook / 'kük / noun
one whose ideas or actions are eccentric, fantastic, . . .

I shouted, *"Fantastic!* I love that word - *fantastic!* Daddy thinks I'm *fantastic!* But what's up with *eccentric?* That word sounds different. Grandma, why is it after readin' the definition for a *new word,* the definition has more *new words* to look up to figure out what the first *new word* meant in the first place?"

Grandma thumbed through the dictionary and commented, "It helps to increase our vocabulary and our intelligence. According to Noah, eccentric means . . ."

---

ec·cen·tric / ik-' sen-trik / *adjective*
1 a : deviating from an established or usual pattern
or style

"Now I'm really confused. What does *that* definition mean?"

Grandma Brombaugh laughed, scratched her head, and explained, "You, my dear, march to the beat of a different drum!"

I crossed my eyes really funny and scratched my head. With a twinkle in her eye, Grandma continued, "Let's just say God broke the mold when He made you. Ronda, you're one of a kind – out of the ordinary – different!"

"No wonder eccentric sounded different – it means different. Grandma, you've always said, 'God made us *all* different.' *Mr. World BookWorm Encyclopedia* told me there are no two people exactly alike. None of us talk alike, walk alike, sound alike, act alike, or think alike – not even twins. Did you know there are no two fingerprints alike?"

"That's right, Ronda. We're all different. But we're alike in many ways. We've all been given the responsibility to share love and joy to make this world a better place. What makes everyone special is that we use our different gifts and talents to do so. Always remember, '*Rays of love and joy fall as sunshine on the heart!*'"

I shouted, "'*Rays of love and joy fall as sunshine on the heart!*' I could be a ray to someone's heart today!"

"You *can* and *will* be a ray but not today. It's time for our bedtime story."

Grandma showed me a book about Noah - not *Noah Webster's Dictionary* - the other Noah. Noah doesn't have a last name. We call him the *Big Boat Man!* Noah is part of the book "*Animals of the Bible.*" Grandma shared that "*Animals of the Bible*" was the first book ever to win a very famous award - the Caldecott in 1938. The Caldecott is given to the best picture book of the year.

"This book came out when your mother was only nine years old. It was one of her favorite books." Grandma said, "There are thirty black and white pictures sketched with a special pencil. Dorothy Lathrop, the illustrator, had a *vivid imagination* and *loved animals*. She wanted the stories in the Old and New Testament to come alive on paper. Dorothy would have the animals come into her studio and sit for her."

"They'd sit down? I can't imagine any of our sheep, pigs, or calves sittin' down long enough to take a picture - let alone draw a picture. Noah sure had some funny lookin' animals and a big beautiful rainbow, too!"

"Animals are all made and shaped differently. Some animals fly, some swim, some hop, some run, and some gallop. They each have a purpose in the animal kingdom. And more importantly, Ronda, *we* have a purpose – to bring rays of . . ."

". . . love and joy to someone's heart!"

As she turned out the light, Grandma said what she always says as she turns out the light: "Sweet dreams - don't let the bedbugs bite!"

I fell asleep smilin'. I woke up laughin'. I had the wildest dream! When I got home and shared my dream with Momma, we both couldn't stop laughin'. We wrote a song. Momma said, "Ronda, what a *vivid imagination* you have. You sure do *love animals*!"

Mrs. Shipley, my piano teacher, smiled from ear to ear when I shared it with her. Rays of love and joy fell as sunshine on her heart. A funny thing happened; the rays came back and fell as sunshine on my heart, too! Get ready for some rays!

Feature Creatures

words and music by R. Friend

feature creatures born with a brilliant mind.

Extraordinary simply put we're one of a kind. Re-

markable, exceptional, fantastic, gifted too, Precious, cherished,

and unique that's me and you! God made you!

God made

God made

15

CHAPTER 2

Spooky!!! Kooky!!! Spooky!!!

Fiddlesticks and gumdrop bars! Where was I? Better yet, where was Diane? I'd looked everywhere in our room. I ran down the stairs shoutin', "Daddy, I can't find Diane anywhere! She's disappeared! She's gone! She's nowhere to be found. I've checked the closets, behind the doors, under the beds . . ."

"Calm down, Ronda, calm down!" Daddy instructed.

We entered the kitchen to join the family meetin'. Arms crossed, Daddy and Ronald leaned up against the washer and dryer. Ronald was enjoyin' a *Dum Dum* lollipop - candy before breakfast again. Doesn't he remember Grandma's advice? - "You are what you eat!"

Duane was holdin' an ice bag over his black eye - the one I gave him yesterday. Although my black eye that Tilly Winks Tilly gave me yesterday is almost gone, Momma handed me a warm washcloth. I saw a tear drop from Momma's eye.

"Let's all remember, patience is the best remedy for trouble," Daddy assured us. "Time and patience helped Duane's and Ronda's black eyes heal. Time and patience will help us find Diane! Besides, Diane has a special guardian angel."

Did he say *guardian angel?* "Where's Grandma Brombaugh?" I asked.

"I just got off the phone with her," replied Momma. "The neighbor is changing a flat tire for her. Grandma said even if she had to fly to get here, she would."

I thought, "*Fly?* Grandma *is* an undercover angel."

Daddy gave us our marchin' orders. "Duane, head to the hayloft! Ronald, run down to the creek."

Duane and Ronald bolted out the front door. They forgot to close the screen door! "Boys, were you born in a barn? Please close the door! Do you want birds flying in?" Momma asked.

Ronald returned and accidentally slammed the door shut. "Sorry, Momma," he hollered.

Momma offered to check the chicken house. Diane loves to collect the green eggs that *Susie Suess* lays. Daddy said, "Don't worry. We'll find her. I'll check the milk house. Diane made a new playhouse for Cotton Ball and her new litter of rabbits. Ronda, have you checked all the nooks and crannies?"

"Nooks 'n crannies are spooky!"

"My little *Kooky*, you've hidden in many of those places yourself. Pretend to be a detective just like on *Dragnet* – one of my favorite radio shows. Help me sing the theme song: 'Dum 'd dum dum! Dum 'd dum dum dum!' Special Detective Ronda Jean, skedaddle! Double check those nooks and crannies. Let's find Diane."

I saluted, "Yes, sir!"

There Daddy goes again - sayin' that I'm *special*. Duane always says I'm *different*. I guess it's just another reason Momma spells my name R-O-N-D-A. Most Rhondas, most *normal* Rhondas, spell their name with an "h."

R-H-O-N-D-A. I'm Ronda *without a honda!* I'll be the first to admit - I am *not* normal. I'm out of the ordinary. I'm Ronda without an "h" because I'm . . .

KOOKY! KOOKY! KOOKY!

If I'm *kooky,* this old farmhouse is *kooky* too! I've never seen another farmhouse like it. It's not only kooky - it's spooky! I ran to our bedroom again to check the attic door. Whew! The attic door was shut, locked, and secured.

I *had* forgotten to check the chest in the window seat. Momma uses it for storage. It would make a great place to hide. I slowly lifted the lid, but no Diane. I did find a hat and several other items. I wanted to know more, but I had to find Diane. I plopped the green hat on my head and continued my search.

Not every house has a laundry chute. But we do. It's upstairs outside our bathroom. One just opens the teeny, tiny door in the wall, throws dirty clothes in the chute, and three stories later, clothes land in a laundry cart in the cellar. We don't use the laundry chute for laundry. Our washer 'n dryer are in the kitchen.

Duane and I use the laundry chute for fun. When Momma's not watchin', we'll throw paper planes or paper dolls down the chute. I would *never* use Chatty Cathy, but we tried my new Barbie doll. Attached to a parachute, we threw her down the chute. Duane and I raced each other to the cellar. Barbie won!

Maybe Diane had decided to hide in the laundry chute. I poked my head in the door but couldn't see a thing. It was as black as burnt toast. *Could she be stuck?* There was one way to find out! I threw my hat down the chute, slid down the banister, charged through the living room, bolted into the kitchen to the back door, and flew down two flights of steps to the cellar.

Whew! I picked up the hat from the laundry cart, wiped off the dust, and placed it on my head. There was the proof. Diane wasn't stuck in the laundry chute. **P.U.!** It was stinky down here. The smell reminded me of Duane's dirty, wet socks. I skedaddled out of there.

As I ran up the cellar stairs, I wondered where *"Miss Hawkephant"* was when I needed her. Diane was nowhere to be found. I started thinking that if only I had a memory like an elephant and eyes like a hawk, I could remember where she loves to hide the most, zoom in, and solve this mystery - just like on *Dragnet*. I started singin', *"Dum 'd dum dum! Dum 'd dum dum dum!"*

Daddy had told me I was a special detective! If I was gonna think like a detective, I needed to look like one. I put on a pair of Ronald's old black glasses, threw Daddy's overcoat on, grabbed a flashlight, picked up a notepad, stuck a pencil behind my ear, and headed to my favorite room - the parlor.

Accordin' to Noah Webster, a parlor is . . .

---

par·lor / pär-l&r / noun
1 : a room used primarily for conversation or the reception of guests: 2 : a room in a private dwelling for the entertainment of guests

---

I call the parlor my *practice* parlor. I'm *practicin'* to entertain guests. I practice singin' in the parlor, I practice playin' the piano in the parlor, I practice dancin' in the parlor, and I practice somersaults and backbends in the parlor. Diane and I play games in the parlor, too. That was it! Maybe Diane was hidin' in here waitin' on me to play games.

I looked behind the couch. I looked behind the piano. I looked behind the two beautiful glass doors that greet guests as they enter the parlor. That'd be a silly place to hide. It's see-through! Diane wasn't there. Where could she be? Maybe she was hidin' in the fireplace.

In the 1850's, the parlor's fireplace was used to heat this house. We don't use it for heat. Daddy says two huge tanks in the cellar, filled with fuel oil, pump heat to registers in every room. He plugged up the hole in the fireplace with a rolled up piece of carpet. That way the cold air in the winter and the hot air from the summer can't come inside.

We use the fireplace once a year for family pictures. Santa uses it once a year for deliveries. On Christmas Eve, a jolly, red giant shoutin', *"Ho, ho, ho,"* slides down our chimney, and the carpet gives way, which cushions Santa's fall. He dusts himself off, stuffs our stockin's, plops presents 'round the tree, reads our letters, scribbles a few notes, and gobbles down cookies 'n milk. The snack gives him enough energy to skedaddle up the chimney to repeat the process – only somewhere else!

Maybe Diane was hidin' in the fireplace. I stuck my head and flashlight up the chimney. *Spooky! Spooky! Spooky!* It was definitely *dark*, *dirty*, and *dusty*. I placed the flashlight under my arm, and with my head stuck in the chimney, I took notes. Well, I drew pictures. I can't write yet. Diane was definitely not in the chimney. The rolled up carpet was still blockin' the openin'. Like any good detective, I kept lookin'. I spied more dust and dirt, cobwebs, and spi . . . Oh, no!

I SPY

SPIDERS !!!!!

SPOOKY SPIDERS!!!!!

SPOOKY KOOKY SPIDERS!!!!!

SPOOKY KOOKY SPOOKY SPIDERS!!!!!

Frightened, I dropped the flashlight. I couldn't see a thing. In order to escape, I ducked my head, but not enough, and hit it on the fireplace. *I was out of there!* I plopped down on my knees, crawled out of the fireplace, jumped to my feet, shook my arms and legs in order to shake the spiders off, bolted out of the parlor, dashed through the living room, slid on the linoleum in the kitchen, burst out the back door, and dashed down two flights of stairs.

CHAPTER 3

Dum 'D Dum Dum!!!

P.U.! My head was spinnin'. Why had I come to the cellar? I looked around for clues. Starin' at the laundry chute, I remembered. I had forgotten to check the closet to the dumbwaiter. *Dum 'd dum dum!* Diane was hidin' in the *dumb*waiter!

Some of my friends don't even know what a *dumbwaiter* is. If you ask me, a dumbwaiter is not so dumb. I think the person who invented the dumbwaiter is even smarter. Accordin' to Noah, a dumbwaiter is

> **dumb·wait·er / 'd&m-"wA-t&r / noun**
> 2 : a small elevator used for conveying food and dishes from one story of a building to another

Every summer, Momma and Grandma fill the dumbwaiter with jars of fruits and vegetables. The dumbwaiter is lowered to the cellar, and the jars are stored in the cellar closet. Whenever we need more fruits and vegetables in the kitchen, we place them in the dumbwaiter down in the cellar, then pull on the pulleys. Moments later, the dumbwaiter appears in the kitchen. What if Diane was hidin' in the dumbwaiter? Once Momma put too many jars in the dumbwaiter, and it fell - kerplunk - all the way to the cellar floor.

Fiddlesticks and gumdrop bars! Maybe Diane's weight lowered the dumbwaiter to the cellar. I opened the dumbwaiter's door. *Surprise!* There was no dumbwaiter - no Diane! I looked up the shaft. It was pitch black. I ran upstairs, opened the door in the kitchen to the dumbwaiter - no Diane - no dumbwaiter. Duane walked into the kitchen. "Duane, did you find Diane?"

"No! What are you doing?"

"I checked for Diane in the dumbwaiter down in the cellar and in the kitchen. I think Diane and the dumbwaiter might be stuck in the middle."

"What are we waiting on?" Duane hollered. *"Help me, Ronda! Help, help me, Ronda!"*

My mind wandered. "'Help me, Ronda! Help, help me, Ronda!' That could make a great song!"

"Concentrate, Ronda, concentrate. Pull up on the cables. Diane could have fallen into the shaft and landed on top of the dumbwaiter!"

We pulled and pulled. I complained, "This dumbwaiter sure is heavy - very heavy!"

Duane commented, "The dumbwaiter, dingbat, might be heavy because Diane . . ."

"*Dingbat! Dingbat!* Duane, did you just call me a '*dingbat?*'"

"Yes, but remember, Ronda, after you hit me over the head with a bat yesterday, you told me I could call you a 'dingbat' whenever I wanted."

I scratched my head and mumbled, "Dumb 'd dumb dumb! What was I thinkin'?"

"Did you just call me 'dumb 'd dumb dumb?'" Duane asked.

"No, Duane. I called myself *'dumb 'd dumb dumb'* for lettin' you call me a *'dingbat.'* For now, let me concentrate on bein' a detective just like on *Dragnet*."

I put my hands to my temples and hummed, **"Dum 'd dum dum!"**

Duane joined in and we chorused, **"Dum 'd dum dum dum!"**

We both struggled with the pulleys. "Ronda, have you ever thought the dumbwaiter might be heavy because Diane is *stuck in the dumbwaiter?"*

We pulled harder and harder. It wouldn't budge. Duane looked down the shaft as Ronald walked in the door still eatin' a *Dum Dum* lollipop. He forgot to latch the door again. Momma wasn't around, so I filled in for her. "Ronald, were you born in a barn? Please close the door! Do you want birds flyin' in?"

Ronald slammed the door shut. I added, "Remember, Ronald, *'you are what you eat'*, so get the *Dum Dum* out of your mouth."

Duane popped his head up from the shaft of the dumbwaiter. "Are you calling me a 'dumb 'd dumb dumb' again?"

I hollered, "I'm not callin' either of you 'dumb 'd dumb dumbs.' I told Ronald to get the *Dum Dum* out of his mouth. Right now I need help with this dumbwaiter. Diane could very well be stuck!"

Ronald offered to help. He insisted it was impossible for Diane to be stuck in the dumbwaiter. We pulled 'n pulled 'n pulled. *Mr. World Book Worm Encyclopedia* was right! There was the dumbwaiter but there was no Diane! Pullin' out more *Dum Dums* from his pocket, Ronald gloated, "I told you so! Diane is too big to fit into a dumbwaiter because of all the shelves! Would either of you care for a *Dum Dum?*"

Frustrated, Duane and I responded at the same time. I shouted, "No, Ronald. I don't want a Dum Dum! I was hopin' Diane was in the dumbwaiter!"

Duane shouted, "Yes, Ronald. I would love a Dum Dum! And you are absolutely right about this dumbwaiter."

When Daddy walked in, he asked, "What are you calling each other?"

Duane and I chorused, "We're detectives, Daddy.

'Dum 'd dum dum. Dum'd dum dum dum!'"

Daddy smiled. Ronald added, "I was just asking if anyone cared for a *Dum Dum*?"

Momma didn't care for a *Dum Dum*. She just wanted to know if we'd found Diane. All three of us shook our heads "no".

CHAPTER 4

The Movin' Monster Blob!

Momma took my hat off and removed some cobwebs. "Ronda, what happened to your head?"

I felt a knot on my forehead. Duane denied doing it. Momma smiled and placed an ice pack on my head this time. Daddy laughed, "There those two go again! Birds of a feather flock together!"

I told them I must have hit my head on the fireplace. "Have you checked every nook and cranny in your room?" Daddy asked.

"Yes. Diane's gone. She's disappeared! What are we gonna do?"

Momma reminded me again that patience is the best remedy for trouble. She suggested we search the bedroom with a fine tooth comb. I knew I'd hit my head, but my baby sister was not so small we'd have to use a comb to find her. So I suggested we just go upstairs and look everywhere one more time.

I, the detective, detected nothin' had changed. "The room is just like I left it. Diane's covers are piled high in a tight wad on her bed. She's not under the bed, she's not in the closet, she's not in the attic, she's not in the chest under the window . . ."

"The co – co – co - covers . . . " Duane stuttered as his eyes bulged in fear. *"Look out! The covers are moving! It's a **MONSTER BLOB!!!**"*

All eyes were focused on the movin' covers. The movin' blob looked like a punchin' bag with somethin' or someone punchin' from the inside tryin' to get out. "It's a **MOVIN' MONSTER BLOB!** Let's get out of here!" I warned.

"Calm down, calm down," cautioned Daddy. "That is not a **MOVIN' MONSTER BLOB!**"

Not only did Daddy touch the blob, he started talkin' to the blob, "Daddy's here. Don't worry, Daddy's here."

Daddy looked at us. "This **MOVIN' BLOB** is your baby sister."

Diane had wrapped herself up in covers so tight, she couldn't even find her way out. Daddy helped her escape. Miss Sleepyhead's head appeared. Diane's hair was tossed and tangled. Her eyes were full of sleepers - the yucky stuff that collects in the corners of your eyes while you're sleepin'.

Diane stretched her arms toward the ceilin', let out a big yawn, opened her eyes, and said, *"What's evwybody lookin' at?"*

Duane, Ronald, and I looked at each other and chorused, *"Ready or not - here we come!"*

We landed in a dog pile on Diane's bed. Momma and Daddy joined us. We laughed until our sides hurt. Grandma appeared out of nowhere in the doorway. "Well, if it isn't six little monkeys jumping on the bed! I flew here as fast as I could to help. But it seems like Diane found you!"

What a coincidence! We found Diane right before the undercover angel flew into the room!

Diane screamed, *"Looky! Monkeys jumpin' on da bed!"*

The rule is no jumpin' on the bed. But today Momma didn't seem to mind! Diane hid one more time as Grandma listened to the Friends sing:

Five little monkeys jumpin'
on the bed!
Where's Diane - Miss Sleepyhead? Wrapped up in covers -
our little mummy!
Tickle her armpits, toes, and tummy!

Six little monkeys jumpin' on the bed!
One, two, three - we all bump heads!
Six little monkeys - birds of a feather -
Friends all happy to be together!

Daddy hollered, "Did someone mention feathers? One, two, three –
pillow fight!!!"

CHAPTER 5

My Daddy — An American Hero!

After the pillow fight was over, we sat down to rest. Momma took a warm washcloth to Diane's sleepers as I plopped the hat back on my head. "Ronda, where did you find that hat?" Daddy asked.

"In the chest of the window seat - whose is it?"

"It's Daddy's army hat. He's a hero," Duane answered.

"Of course Daddy's a hero!" I agreed. "He helped Diane escape from the covers!"

Everyone laughed.

"Whatsa he-woe?" Diane whispered.

We laughed harder and chorused, "HERO, DIANE. HERO!!!"

Grandma opened up the dictionary. According to Noah, a hero is . . .

---

he·ro / ʽhir-(ʺ)O / ʽhE-(ʺ)rO / *noun*
c : a man admired for his achievements and noble qualities; d : one that shows great courage

---

Ronald explained, "Soldiers are heroes - strong and brave! Daddy was an American hero in World War II."

With goo-goo eyes, Momma shared, "Daddy doesn't brag about his accomplishments – most heroes don't."

Momma walked over to the window seat and pulled out a picture of a very handsome soldier in uniform, a medal shaped like a star, and a small journal. Meanwhile, Ronald stood at attention, saluted, and barked, "Daddy was a sergeant for the Black Cats, 24th Tank Battalion. In 1942 the soldiers trained for over two years at Camp Bowie in Texas and Camp Beale in California. According to the World Book Encyclopedia, tanks 'formed the spearheads in the successful Allied drives across France toward Germany.'"

Mr. BookWorm continued, "January 1945 - Daddy's division traveled first by train, then by ship. Sergeant Harold Eugene Friend was a tank commander. Under his command were four other soldiers – a driver, an assistant driver, a loader, and a gunner. For seven months the 24th Tank Battalion traveled 1,608 miles through France, Germany, and Austria, fighting battles to save lives and provide freedom."

"Jean," whispered Grandma, "*Mr. BookWorm* could talk for hours. Tell the girls the doll story."

"At ease, Ronald," Momma ordered. "Your father kept this small journal – a Notizbuch – meaning "notebook" in German. Daddy wrote, '. . . we ended up near Kassel about eleven miles from the front. We bedded ourselves down in a large mansion. . . . Our loader, John Miller, could play the piano, and by pure luck our room had a beautiful one sitting in the corner. . . . I wish I could have had a picture of the room that night. We set the table with everything we could find including candles. It looked so nice. We invited Lt. Harvey for supper. John Geiger of Pittsburg was our chief cook.'"

Daddy interrupted to tell us they ate beans for dinner. We laughed. Momma continued readin', "'[The mansion] was the place where I found our little blond doll. We had the little doll ever since and it has been our good luck charm. I gave it to my gunner – Ray Schlee of Buffalo, New York . . . in hopes that he can take it home to his little daughter, Sandy.'"

". . . and he did!" Daddy whispered as a tear fell from his cheek.

"Daddy took on the responsibility to see that his tank crew returned home safely to America. He wanted their dreams to come true."

Ronald saluted and barked again, "The Black Cats arrived back home in the United States on July 23, 1945, for a special dinner – steaks, vegetables, fresh fruits, milk, and ice cream."

"No beans," Daddy laughed.

Momma smiled. "Today your father looks after the Friend family. Daddy protects you, provides for you, watches over you, cares for you, and loves you more than you'll ever know."

"Daddy makes rays of love and joy fall like sunshine."

"Your daddy also gave his friend, Ray, hope. Each of us can be a ray of hope," added Momma as she picked up the medal star.

"It's a bronze star!" Duane shouted.

"What did you do, Daddy?" I asked.

"I did what any friend would do for his friend."

Ronald boasted, "Daddy, not just any friend would save three other men by putting his own life in danger. The European war ended on May 7, 1945. Daddy received his bronze medal near the picturesque town of Neu Otting."

Ronald read Daddy's Bronze Medal Citation. After he was finished, Daddy added, "I was proud to be an American soldier. Whether you become a soldier, teacher, doctor, nurse, lawyer, astronaut, scientist, or farmer, we all have a common mission - *to help our friends make it through the battles of everyday life.* That's what heroes do!"

Diane muttered, *"Daddy, I wanna be a he-woe, too!"*

"Me too," I shouted. "I want to share rays of love, joy, and hope that will fall like sunshine on someone's heart!"

Momma responded, "Ronda, I have the perfect someone!"

CHAPTER 6

A Little Sunshine for Sunshine!

The girls went to the kitchen to fix breakfast. The boys headed outside to feed the livestock. They forgot to latch the screen door *again*. **Fiddlesticks and gumdrop bars!** "Boys, were you born in a barn? Please close the door! Do you want birds flying in?" Momma sighed.

Duane quickly returned to shut the door. "No, Momma. No siree!"

Momma's face looked troubled. And it wasn't about the door. She told me that LeAnne Taylor, a farmer's daughter across the cornfield, needed a little sunshine. I was confused. LeAnne's nickname is Sunshine. She's always happy. "Why does Sunshine need sunshine?" I asked.

"Recently her family found out that Sunshine has cancer."

"What's cancer?"

Momma didn't have to look that word up in the dictionary. She'd studied to be a nurse before she met Daddy. "Cancer is a disease that fights to destroy your body. Bad cells fight to take over the good cells in your body."

"Like a battle?"

"That's a good way to put it. Sunshine is strong. But she's only eight. The treatments to fight the cancer are hard on the body. They take away your energy. Sunshine needs plenty of rest. Her body needs to concentrate on getting better."

Grandma whispered, "Doctors and nurses help heal sick bodies. They're heroes too! The best thing we can do now is to remember Sunshine in our thoughts and prayers. *I believe in miracles!*"

Momma added, "It takes a lot of hard work and dedication to be a doctor or nurse. They'll do everything they can to see that Sunshine's dreams come true. Grandma and I both wanted to be nurses, but it wasn't meant to be."

"Grandma, you studied to be a nurse, too?"

"Yes, but when your grandpa died, I needed to go to work to make a living. I couldn't afford to go to school and take care of your mother."

"You can imagine how excited Grandma was when I entered nursing school. But it wasn't meant to be, either. I met your father at church, and we fell in love. I didn't finish school."

"What does fallin' in love have to do with not finishin' school?" I was confused.

Grandma explained, "The rule at the nursing school was that one couldn't be married and go to school at the same time. Your mother chose your father over a nursing career. Several years later the rules changed, and you could be married. But by that time your mother already had her hands full."

The phone rang. Momma answered. It sounded like Sunshine's mother. I told Grandma I had the best parents in the whole wide world! She agreed. Momma hung up. Sunshine's treatments were over. But she needed the next couple of weeks to gain her strength back.

I jumped out of my chair, danced 'round the table, and shouted, "It's time for rays of love, joy, and hope to fall as sunshine on Sunshine's heart!"

Grandma smiled and then looked down at my feet. For a moment, I *thought* the undercover angel thought *I* was an angel too! She was checkin' to see if my feet were off the ground.

Momma suggested, "Let's make a *Sunshine Basket* for 'Miss Sunshine' herself!"

"How we gonna ketch da shunshine?" asked Diane.

Everyone laughed! Momma must have known by the look on my face that I didn't know what a *Sunshine Basket* was, either. She explained, "A *Sunshine Basket* is a huge basket filled with everything **under the sun** that will bring a ray of love, joy, and hope - small presents, encouraging notes, funny jokes, and food. The purpose is that everything - handmade or store bought - brings **sunshine to the heart!** Why don't the two of you go upstairs to the extra bedroom and pick out the biggest basket you can find?"

Diane and I raced out of the kitchen. We were neck 'n neck in the livin' room. Roundin' the stairs, my foot . . .

"Ronda Jean Friend!"

Diane fell, hit her chin, and bit her tongue. She was cryin' like a baby but quit cryin' long enough to say, *"Wonda did it on porpoise!"*

Here we go again. I decided to take a shortcut. "It wasn't an accident. I did it on purpose – not *porpoise* – and Momma, I'm sorry. I was so excited about the *Sunshine Basket*. I wanted to make it to the top first, so I tripped Diane with my foot."

Diane interrupted me. *"Momma, I got a booboo!*
Two big booboos,"
she cried, pointin' to her knee and chin.

Diane's such a baby. There was a teeny, tiny spot of blood. Momma pulled Band-aids from her apron pocket and put them on Diane's booboos! I gave my sister a hug, swallowed my pride, and apologized. "Diane, I'm really sorry. I just wanted to beat you - not hurt you. All I wanted to do is spread rays of love, joy, and hope like sunshine on someone's heart. I guess I should have started with you! You can pick out Sunshine's basket. I'll go to my time-out chair. Momma, I promise I won't move."

I turned back and shouted, "Grandma, I'm sorry. I'm *not* an angel."

Under her breath, Grandma whispered, **"Not yet!"**

Momma scratched her head. She headed back to the kitchen hummin' her new favorite song - "Put on a Happy Face" - from the new musical "Bye Bye Birdie!" I have no idea what birds have to do with a happy face. But it gave me a great idea. I'd write a new song!

PUT ON A SMILEY FACE!

Know someone who's all shook up?
Put on a smiley face.
Have a friend who needs cheered up?
Put on a smiley face.

Take some time to show you really care.
Go the second mile!
Spread joy and laughter everywhere
Help someone don a smile!

Pick out some presents – surprise
Someone who's down and out!
You can even do it in disguise!
That's what love's all about!

Just spread sunshine all over the place!
Put a smile on someone else's face.

Put on a smiley face. Put on a smiley face.

Don't feel sad anymore.
Don't sit alone and whine.
Think of all you're thankful for –
Let rays of joy fall as sunshine!

Care! Sow seeds of kindness.
Spread some love around.
The best reward in life is
Seeing frowns turned upside down!

So spread Sunshine Baskets all over the place
And you'll make a happy, You'll see a smiley,
You'll make a happy, joyful, cheerful,
gleeful, smiley face!

Time's up for time-out.

I invited my guests into the parlor for some entertainment. You can't keep from smilin' while singin' that song! Momma smiled. Grandma smiled. Diane smiled. Even Teeny and Tiny were listenin' outside on the front porch and wouldn't quit barkin'. I think they liked it!

I spun around to take a bow, slipped on the carpet, stood up, hit my head on the fireplace, tried to catch myself, fell to the ground, and skinned my knee on the carpet. "FIDDLESTICKS & GUMDROP BARS! I'm bleeding! I'M BLEEDING!!! I have a big booboo - a really BIG, **BIG** **BOOBOO** on my knee - and one on my noggin, too!"

Momma gave me a big hug, kissed my forehead, and went to pull out more Band-aids from her apron. They were all gone. Grandma handed Momma a hanky. She always has hankies in her pocket. Momma instructed, "Ronda, put pressure on your knee with this hanky. The bleeding will stop in a minute."

Momma winked at Grandma. Grandma winked back. That's a sure sign they have somethin' up their sleeves. Momma shared, "Remember, accidents happen. You've been so busy playing detective and songwriter - haven't you forgotten something from last night?"

"*Fiddlesticks and gumdrop bars!* You're gonna tell me what fiddlesticks and gumdrop bars are!"

Momma entertained us in the parlor by recitin' the rest of the poem.

Fiddlesticks and gumdrop bars –
Doesn't matter where you are!
Accidents happen – don't come unglued –
Smile – it's all in your attitude.

Cry over spilled milk? Now don't get upset!
Think of sweet blessings – don't you forget!
What matters most is family and friends.
Down on Friendly Acres – love never ends!

What can Fiddlesticks and Gumdrop Bars be?
They're delicious desserts for precious tummies!
So when you're old with grandchildren galore –
May this precious moment live on evermore!

A lesson for heart, body, and soul –
There are some things in life we have no control.
Accidents happen – Wow! Sometimes they hurt!
Sit yourself down and enjoy some dessert!

Fiddlesticks and gumdrop bars –
Doesn't matter where you are!
Accidents happen – don't come unglued –
Smile – it's all in your attitude.

FIDDLESTICKS AND GUMDROP BARS!

"Desserts – how sweet is that?"

"They're very sweet," Momma said. "I'll race you to the kitchen!"

"I'd better not," I laughed. "I don't want to trip you!"

Sittin' at the kitchen table, I discovered that Momma and Grandma Brombaugh had done a little detective work, too. Momma accidentally had misplaced these recipes years ago. They'd practically tore the kitchen apart lookin' in every nook 'n cranny for these long lost recipes. They'd found them!

Momma gathered ingredients while Grandma shared, "My mother, Ida Peters, would make these desserts for your mother when accidents happened. Grandma Peters loved fiddlesticks. Some people call them haystacks, but Grandma loved the fiddle. To her, these desserts looked like stacks of bows for a fiddle – fiddlesticks!"

There was one missin' ingredient for the gumdrop bars. Momma made us guess. Diane and I put our heads together, then whispered in Grandma's ears, "Mbmlblbmm!" (I'd tell you what it is, but then it wouldn't be a secret anymore.)

"I've hidden the secret ingredient," teased Momma. "Let's play the hot and cold game! Girls, you're both cold."

Diane and I held hands and headed to the back porch. Momma warned us that we were gettin' colder and colder. We turned back towards the stove. Maybe it was in the oven. We were still cold. We crawled under the kitchen table and headed for the washer 'n dryer. "You're getting warm!"

We checked inside the washer 'n dryer. There was nothin'. Momma kept sayin' that we were gettin' warmer. Then a light went off in my head – the dumbwaiter! Diane stood on her tiptoes and opened the door. The secret ingredient was hidin' at the top. As I reached for it, a jar accidentally fell and hit me on the head.

Lights blinked off 'n on in my head. But this time when I opened my eyes, I thought I saw a nurse's cap on Momma's head. Nurse Momma came to the rescue again. I rubbed my head, forgot about the pain, and shouted, "It's time for some *fiddlesticks and gumdrop bars!*"

FIDDLESTICKS

1/2 cup peanut butter
6 oz. package of butterscotch chips
1 – 3 oz. can of chow mein noodles
2 cups mini marshmallows

Mix peanut butter and chips in saucepan – melt on low heat.
Add noodles and marshmallows.
Drop on wax paper and chill.

GUMDROP BARS

4 eggs   1/2 t salt
2 cups brown sugar   1 t cinnamon
1 T cold water   1/2 cup nuts
2 cups flour   1 cup gumdrops

Beat eggs until light and fluffy. Add sugar and water and beat again. Sift flour with salt and cinnamon. Sprinkle the candy with a little of it. Add remainder of flour to egg mixture and fold in candy. Spread thin in greased pan and bake at 325 degrees.

While warm, ice with this mixture:

3 T butter
2 T orange juice
Powdered sugar to spread

CHAPTER 7

From the Bottom of My Heart!

The next few days were spent makin' presents and wrappin' them for Sunshine's *Sunshine Basket*. The boys built her a birdhouse. Momma sewed Sunshine a new outfit. Diane made her beautiful flowers out of wire and Kleenex. Momma helped me make pretty, pink slippers out of washcloths.

Daddy and the boys were outside haulin' manure - not a fun job but a big part of farm life. I stood on my stool helpin' Momma with the dishes. "Do you have any idea what Grandma's makin' for Sunshine?"

My question was interrupted. A car pulled into the driveway. I looked out the window, jumped off the stool, and flew out the door. Momma hollered, "Ronda, were you born in a barn? Please close the door! Do you want birds flying in?"

"No, Momma. Sorry," I apologized, shut the door, and ran down the sidewalk to greet Grandma.

"What did you make for Sunshine?"

"Aren't you forgetting something?" she asked as she knelt down for a big bear hug. Grandma whispered in my ear, "One of my gifts is a painting."

Sittin' down at the kitchen table, she revealed her artwork. It was a beautiful butterfly, restin' on a sunflower, which overlooked a frog sittin' on a lily pad. Grandma read the words printed on the frame – *"Sunshine or rain, always and forever, dare to dance, and leap for joy!"* She added, *"Always remember, presents put a smile on a face for a day, but kind words bring love, joy, and hope to the heart forever!"*

Grandma's gift reminded Momma of the most important part of the *Sunshine Basket – from the bottom of my heart* notes! Grandma Brombaugh had started this tradition. When Momma was little, Grandma would leave special notes in her lunchbox, 'specially after Grandpa Brombaugh died. Almost anybody can read them. The sentences are made up of letters, numbers, small words, and pictures. They're special 'cause they come from the deepest part of your heart. Sunshine would love them.

The boys finished haulin' manure and popped their heads in the screen door. P.U.! Grandma caught them just in time. "Boys, are your boots dirty?"

I wanted to say, **"Dirty?** What do you think, Grandma? They've been out feedin' the cows, sloppin' the hogs, and standin' in manure. **Dirty? I think so!"** But I didn't, 'cause yesterday I'd learned that sometimes you need to think before you speak. Besides, the boys both nodded, then slammed the door but it didn't shut.

"Boys, were you born in a barn? Please close the door! Do you want birds flying in?" Momma asked.

As far as I know, none of us was *born in a barn,* and we've *never, ever* had birds fly into the kitchen. The boys shut the door, cleaned up and joined in.

"Momma, we're havin' more fun puttin' this *Sunshine Basket* together than Sunshine will have gettin' it."

Momma smiled. "That's because it's always better to give than to receive!"

I had thought Grandma had all the wisdom. Momma was turnin' into quite an angel herself. *"Miss Hawkephant"* jumped – I mean *flew* – from her seat and ran out of the kitchen! I followed her and hollered back, "Don't worry, Momma! I'll keep a hawk's eye on her!"

I followed Diane up the stairs to our room. I hid in the hallway. Playin' *"Miss Detective"* again, I stood behind our bedroom door, peekin' through the crack. Diane whispered to her baby doll, gave it a long, humongous hug, and darted out the door.

Doll in one hand, Diane plopped her bottom down on the top step, then popped down step by step on her bottom. The Friend Family calls it the *bottom bumpin' boogie.* I tiptoed down the stairs. Daddy came in from finishin' his chores as Diane skipped in the kitchen, handed the doll to Momma, and said, *"I wanna give my baby doll to Shunshine."*

"That's Chatty Baby, your favorite doll. Are you sure?" Momma asked.

"I wanna help Shunshine get bedder. She can give this baby doll to her baby girl one day. I wanna give my fwend wuv and hope! It's fwum da boddum of my heart," Diane shared as she pulled the baby doll to her chest.

Grandma Brombaugh's prayers were being answered. She was turnin' my baby sister into an angel. That was Diane's favorite doll. I would *never* have thought of givin' Chatty Cathy away. I *hafta* admit, I admired my baby sister for her act of kindness.

The *Sunshine Basket* was almost complete! Daddy's mother was the one who'd taught Momma all about *Sunshine Baskets*. Grandma Friend had died when I was only one and a half. Everybody had loved Grandma Friend. She would make hero hats for everyone who helped make *Sunshine Baskets*.

Grandma Friend had believed you didn't have to be someone famous, or rich, or really smart to be a hero - you just had to be kind and treat other people like you would want to be treated. Grandma Brombaugh reminded us, "Noah's definition of a hero is one who is 'admired for his achievements and qualities!' Grandma Friend would say you were all heroes in her book!"

Momma grabbed yesterday's paper, dated April 25, 1961. While makin' our hero hats, I couldn't get the other definition of a hero out of my mind - "one that shows great courage."

CHAPTER 8

Sunshine's Sunshine Basket!

The phone rang. It was Mrs. Taylor. Sunshine was strong enough for a visit. **Get ready for some rays!**

After lunch I helped Daddy plant our garden. The rows in our garden are straight as an arrow. That's 'cause Daddy and I plant stakes at each end, then stretch string from stake to stake. With the string as our guide, we make small holes in the dirt, drop seeds, and cover them with more dirt.

We have some of the richest soil. I reckon it's 'cause we use cow manure. Some parents don't let their kids play in dirt - let alone play in dirt with cow manure mixed in! Farmers know there's somethin' 'bout gettin' your hands dirty and knowin' you've done your part in helpin' things grow.

In our garden we grow everythin' *under the sun.* (Which, by the way, is a great place to grow a garden. Gardens don't do well in the shade!) We grow green beans, peas, lima beans, tomatoes, potatoes, strawberries, cucumbers, onions, lettuce, cauliflower, broccoli, radishes, rhubarb, beets, asparagus, muskmelons, watermelons, squash, zucchini, and sweet corn. Daddy ends up givin' half of it away. He says, "If we do the planting, the Good Lord does the growing, so we can do the giving!"

The lights blinked off and on in my head. I had an idea – a fantastic surprise for Sunshine! I whispered my secret in Daddy's ear. He picked me up in the air, swung me around, and shouted, "My little Kooky, what a fantastic surprise! What are we waiting on?"

We gathered some supplies and snuck off to work. Back just in time for supper, Daddy and I washed our hands in the back sink. Momma hollered, *"What have you two been up to?"*

Daddy winked, smiled, and responded, *"A secret surprise for us to know and you to find out!"*

Daddy's such a joker. He didn't want the secret to accidentally pop out of our heads. When we came to dinner, Daddy and I ate with clothespins on our ears and noses. Our mouths kept busy eatin' our favorites - roast beef, mashed potatoes, corn, and coleslaw. Everyone tried to guess, but we weren't about to tell our secret.

That evenin' the Friends paid a visit to the neighbors down the road. The *Sunshine Basket* was so big that it took Ronald, Duane, and me to carry it. Mrs. Taylor greeted us at the door. Her jaw dropped to the floor. Choked up, Mrs. Taylor spoke, "Thank you. We couldn't have better neighbors!"

Mrs. Taylor warned us that Sunshine didn't look like herself. The treatments made her lose all her hair, so Sunshine wore a hat. Mr. Taylor and Sunshine's brother, Kirk, appeared in the doorway wearin' hats, too! Takin' their hats off, Kirk explained, "We didn't want Sunshine to feel all alone. *We shaved our heads, too!*"

Diane and I giggled.

Headin' to the bedroom, Mrs. Taylor told us that even before her illness, Sunshine was very sensitive to light. She insisted on not openin' the drapes to let the sunshine in until she was all better.

Daddy and I winked at each other. That was gonna make her surprise even more special. We waited outside the bedroom. Mrs. Taylor asked, "Hey, Sunshine! How are you feeling?"

"Honestly, I've felt better," she replied.

"Close your eyes, Sunshine. You have a surprise!"

Sunshine was lyin' in her bed readin' a book. She looked different. I liked her straw hat, although it seemed to be missin' somethin'. Daddy and Momma held the basket while we hid behind it. Mrs. Taylor told her to open her eyes. Four Friends popped out from behind the basket, shoutin', "Surprise! Here's a *Sunshine Basket* for Sunshine!"

Sunshine's eyes popped out as big as saucers when she saw the huge basket overflowin' with presents and cards. "That's for me? All of it?"

"All of it!" Ronald responded. "May this *Sunshine Basket* be like *rays of love, joy, and hope falling like sunshine on your heart*!"

"There's one gift for every day this month," Duane added. "The fun part is that you get to pick which one to open first."

Momma said, "And the baskets will keep comin' until you are all better!"

"Can I open one right now?"

Daddy joked, "If you don't, I will!"

Sunshine's first present was Grandma's painting. She smiled and read, "Sunshine or rain, always and forever, dare to dance, and leap for joy!"

Grandma reminded Sunshine that the Good Lord, the doctors, the nurses, her family, and her friends were all there for her. Placin' a small bottle wrapped in one of her fancy handkerchiefs on Sunshine's nightstand, she instructed, "I recommend a small dose of this several times a day."

"*Momma, Momma!*" Diane whispered.

Diane was holdin' onto Momma's dress with one hand and her baby doll with the other. Momma took her hand, knelt down beside her, and whispered in her ear. Diane smiled and stepped over to the bed.

65

"Shunshine, I want you to have my baby doll. She's a gooood baby. She never cwies. When you look at her, weemember I'll be pwayin' for you."

Sunshine gave Diane a big hug and whispered in her ear, "I'll take good care of her. When I'm better, you can have her back!"

Diane looked up at Momma and smiled. I wanted Sunshine to know about my secret, but then it wouldn't be a secret anymore! "Would anyone like some tea and cookies?" Mrs. Taylor asked.

"Only if you let us help," Grandma said. The women and men headed to the kitchen.

Ronald, Duane, and Kirk went outside to play *Whiffleball*. Diane and I stayed with Sunshine. I wanted to know more about Grandma's secret surprise, but I noticed somethin' just as interestin'. "What book are you readin'?"

"It's '*Where the Wild Things Are.*' It won the Caldecott Award."

"*The* cOw got caught award?" Diane blurted. "*Where did the cow get caught?*"

Sunshine and I laughed. "No, Diane. Not the *Cow Got Caught Award*, the *Caldecott Award* - it's an award given to the best picture book of the year. Grandma showed me the first award book - '*Animals of the Bible.*' Sunshine, your book looks *spooky* and *scary*. Why would anyone want to read a spooky, scary monster book?"

"One might think it's spooky and scary," Sunshine responded. "It's really a story of a little boy with a very vivid imagination who gets sent to bed without supper. Momma gave this book to me to help me understand my illness. The disease I have is a little scary, sort of like the '*wild things.*' But just like the little boy in the book, I don't need to be afraid. Let me read it."

Diane and I crawled up in bed. Sunshine had us make a funny monster face and freeze every time she read, "*Wild thing!*" We laughed. Finished with the story, Sunshine explained, "I don't have to be afraid. No matter what happens, my family will *always* be here for me."

Diane said,
"Weed it again! Pwease! Weed it again!"

Sunshine did. We laughed and laughed. Before Diane could say, "*Weed it again!*" I asked, "Sunshine, aren't you the least bit curious about what's in the handkerchief?"

"You bet I am!"

Sunshine read the note first. "Laughter doeth good like a medicine!"

Grandma had given her a bottle of laughter with the instructions, "Take as often as needed!" Two huge tears fell from Sunshine's face. Diane wiped them away with Chatty Baby's apron. *"Don't cwy! Shunshine, don't cwy!"*

"These aren't sad tears – they're happy tears! My parents, my doctors, my nurses, and now your grandma have all told me the same thing. 'Laughter doeth good like a medicine!' I've laughed more tonight than I have laughed in a long time. I haven't felt this good in weeks."

"Let's laugh sum more! Weed it again!" Diane insisted.

While Sunshine was readin', Mrs. Taylor and Grandma walked in with tea and cookies. Mrs. Taylor commented, "My, my, Sunshine, I haven't seen you smile and laugh like this in days."

"I guess 'laughter doeth good like a medicine!'" Sunshine smiled and winked.

Grandma winked. I winked back!

Daddy promised Sunshine that when her battle was over, we would all gather back in Sunshine's room to celebrate. Diane and I promised Sunshine that we would stop for a visit every other day until then.

CHAPTER 9

Secret in the Garden!

Summer is a busy time on the farm. We can and freeze fruits and vegetables from the garden. Daddy and the boys bale hay, plow the fields, and get ready for the county fair. Daddy loves to enter his alfalfa hay and corn. Ronald and Duane show pigs, cattle, and sheep. Grandma takes her famous angel food cake and homemade egg noodles. Momma works on a few surprises. And Diane and I are too little to enter any contest.

Week after week, Daddy and I would sneak away from the house to work on our secret surprise. And as promised, every other day Diane and I walked through our cornfield to visit Sunshine.

Sometimes we would sing. We picked our favorite songs on the radio. Mine was *"Summertime, Summertime"* – mainly 'cause it was summertime. One day I sang *"Put on a Smiley Face."* Sunshine did. But the song that really made Sunshine smile was a song that was played over and over on the radio -*"He's Got the Whole World in His Hands."* My baby sister's favorite song was *"Rockin' Robin."* She liked it when the robin went "Tweet, tweet, tweet!" All those songs made us want to dance.

So sometimes we would dance. We'd do the bunny hop, the hokey-pokey, square dance, and this new dance called the twist.

Every day Sunshine kept gettin' better 'n better. *And* she grew more hair.

Sometimes we'd take a picnic lunch to the creek and catch tadpoles, or skip rocks, or pick four leaf clovers, or stretch blades of grass in between our thumbs and blow just right to make a whistle sound. Sunshine would always wear her hat to protect her from the sun's rays.

Every day Sunshine kept gettin' better 'n better. *And* she grew more hair.

Sometimes we'd play games. If Sunshine had enough energy, we would jump rope, play hopscotch, or do tricks with our hula hoops. If she needed her rest, we'd play *Twiddlywinks* or *Old Maid*. One day, we hid Diane's baby bunnies in a basket and snuck them into Sunshine's bedroom.

Every day Sunshine kept gettin' better 'n better. *And* she grew more hair.

Sometimes, but not very often, we'd watch the television box. When Momma was a little girl, she didn't watch television. That's because there *were* no televisions. She listened to the radio. Momma warns us we could hurt our eyes if we watch too much television. Mrs. Taylor warns us not to sit too close, or it could hurt our eyes. With all those warnin's, I'd better start watchin' television with my eyes halfway closed.

Sometimes we'd watch *"Bozo the Clown."* Diane loved *"Captain Kangaroo."* We all loved *"I Love Lucy."* They'd just started showin' a really funny nighttime cartoon called *"The Flintstones."* The television box made us laugh. Grandma always says, *"Laughter doeth good like a medicine!"*

Every day Sunshine kept gettin' better 'n better. *And* she grew more hair.

Every day without fail, Sunshine would open another present from the *Sunshine Basket* and a *from the bottom of the heart* note. And every day without fail, Diane and I made sure she took her medicine - a couple of big tablespoons of laughter!

Today Sunshine opened another present from Grandma Brombaugh – a beautiful, crocheted angel named *Faith* and some *kind words.*

Sunshine began to cry. I asked, "Why are you cryin'?"

"I've kept my secret long enough," Sunshine explained. "I was scared when the doctors told me that sometimes people with cancer never get better. They told me that when you go to school, you need to concentrate on the three R's – *reading, 'riting 'n 'rithmetic*. And when you're sick, it's important to concentrate on the three F's – *family, faith, 'n friends*."

I blurted out, "I reckon that's good advice for all of us all of the time!"

Then I patted my head to see if I had grown a halo! Sunshine continued, "I'm nervous. I go to the doctors tomorrow. They'll tell me if the cancer is out of my body. I don't feel like an angel, but I do feel so much better than I did."

"You might not feel like an angel," I said, "but you remind me of one! You make everyone around you smile. Besides, you *have* a guardian angel. Don't forget, Sunshine, '*Sunshine or rain, always and forever, dare to dance, and leap for joy!*' "

Walkin' home through the cornfield, I realized how brave and courageous Sunshine had been. *Sunshine was a hero!*

CHAPTER 10

Hats Off
to Heroes!

It was suppertime. Daddy kept givin' *goo-goo eyes* to Momma. He got up from his chair, went to his closet, and brought back a present. It wasn't even her birthday! Momma was so surprised. She read the note first.

Momma opened her present as Daddy spoke. "Many years ago, your mother was very brave and courageous. She laid aside her dream of becoming a nurse to help the four of you fulfill your dreams. I love and admire her for that. Today it's 'hats off to my hero' – Momma Jean Friend!"

Momma loved her new nurse's cap. Hat in place, Momma proclaimed, "I'll have plenty of time to be a nurse after my family is grown. I love being the Friends' private nurse!"

Momma glowed. She didn't take her nurse's hat off the rest of the night. Daddy even wore his hat as they tucked me into bed. I wrapped my arms 'round their necks and announced, "My momma is my hero for bein' the best private nurse in the whole wide world. My daddy is my hero for watchin' 'n protectin' 'n keepin' his family safe. And my friend, Sunshine, is my hero for facin' a battle with great courage."

We prayed a little extra that night for Sunshine. Then we sang, "He's got a whole lot of Sunshine in His hands. He's got a whole lot of Sunshine . . ."

Bright 'n early the next mornin', we were puttin' up corn. Grandma sharpened her knives. The boys finished pullin' 'n shuckin' the corn from the garden. Shuckin' corn makes for lots of shucks. The boys quickly threw all the shucks into the cattle trough – and just in time. Clouds rolled in. We were in for a little rain.

In the kitchen, huge pots filled with water were boilin' on the stove. Momma dumped the ears in the water. Meantime, I filled the sinks up with very cold water and added ice. When the corn was finished cookin', Momma strained the water off in the back sink and placed the ears in the ice cold water. When Grandma could touch the corn without burnin' her hands off, she'd cut the corn off the ear. By the time Diane and I spooned the cut corn into containers for the freezer, we had ourselves a summer rain.

Diane and I laid down for a nap after lunch. I couldn't sleep. I kept thinkin' 'bout Sunshine. The phone rang. I snuck halfway down the stairs to listen. Momma said, "That's wonderful news! I'll let everyone know!"

"Everyone know what?" I yelled as I did the Friends' *bottom bumpin' boogie* down the rest of the way.

Momma didn't seem to mind that I was missin' out on my nap. She was jumpin' up 'n down.

"I've got great news! Sunshine's body is free of any cancer cells! *She's in remission!*"

I started jumpin' up 'n down too. I didn't know what "remission" meant, but whatever it meant, it must have been good. Momma added, "They want us to come over tonight for the party! Sunshine has a surprise!"

Sunshine had a surprise? So did I! The rain stopped. I ran outside to tell Daddy the good news. It took us two full hours to put the finishin' touches on our surprise. By the time we finished, we were a **sight for sore eyes**. We snuck down to the cellar to clean up before anybody could see just how messy we were.

Daddy and Momma were in one of their silly moods. I pretended to look up their sleeves. Daddy, the joker, said, "You think we have something up there?"

"I do! Is it a surprise for Sunshine?"

They laughed and chanted,

"For us to know and you to find out!"

Momma added, "Now Ronda, don't you and Daddy have a surprise that I don't know about?"

She had a point!

As promised months ago, the party was in Sunshine's bedroom. It was rainin' on the outside. But there was plenty of sunshine on the inside.

Sunshine looked beautiful dressed in the new outfit Momma had made for her – a brown, smocked top with a petaled, yellow skirt. She wore green shoes, and it reminded me of my surprise! Mrs. Taylor announced that it was time for Sunshine's surprise. "Sunshine, the stage is all yours!"

Sunshine stood. "First of all, thanks for three months worth of *Sunshine Baskets*. I loved them all. You've all taught me, **'Presents put a smile on a face for a day, but kind words bring love, joy, and hope to the heart forever!'**

May these kind words return a little of the love, joy, and hope you've given me."

Hats Off To Heroes

There's Superman, Zorro, Fantastic Four,
Lone Ranger, Popeye, heroes galore,
The Incredible Hulk, Batman and Robin,
Mighty Mouse, Spiderman with one thing in common!

They're magical - make believe - all in our dreams.
Save the World! Save the Day! - their common theme.
To cheer us up when we're feelin' blue -
In our everyday life we need heroes too!

Doctors and nurses, fathers and mothers,
Coaches, teachers, sisters, and brothers,
Soldiers, pastors, rabbis, and grandpas,
Policemen, firemen, neighbors, and grandmas.

No matter their title, there's one common thread.
They're our special hero - a forever friend.
When we seem to be at the end of our rope
Heroes plant seeds of love, joy, and hope!

You've done it for me - Yes, Sunshine's my name!
You've brightened my world - I'm not the same!
Doctors say, "A miracle! You've been blessed!"
"Laughter's like medicine," I confessed!

Friends, thanks for the basket full of sunshine,
"From the bottom of my heart," I feel love divine!
Rays of love, joy, and hope - great works of art -
Fell down like sunshine on my grateful heart!

Your Forever Friend!
Sunshine

Everyone stood. Everyone applauded. Everyone cried. Grandma ran out of hankies so Mrs. Taylor grabbed a tissue box. Sunshine went over to Diane and handed her Chatty Baby. "Diane, I promised."

"Tanks, Shunshine!"

"No, Diane, **tank** *you!*"

Daddy motioned for me to join him. "Ronda and I have been working on a little surprise, too."

I blurted out, "We even had to mow down several rows of corn this afternoon!"

Daddy continued, "Sunshine, months ago you didn't want to open your curtains to let the light shine in until your battle was over. **Sunshine, let the sunshine in!**"

Daddy pulled the curtain wide open to unveil our surprise. In the midst of our huge cornfield was a magnificent field of sunflowers in full bloom. But Daddy and I got a surprise, too. The rain had stopped, the sun had come out, and a double rainbow had appeared above the sunflowers.

"They're beautiful - absolutely beautiful," Sunshine shouted.

Daddy pulled a sunflower from a paper sack. Momma pinned it on Sunshine's hat. I shared, "Daddy taught me all about sunflowers. Sunshine, you remind us of a sunflower! Thanks to Momma, you even look like one.

Sunflowers always follow the sunlight, never turnin' their back on the sun. Even after takin' a beatin' durin' a storm, they'll stand strong with their heads held high lookin' up towards the sun. Sunshine, thanks for bein' a sunflower!"

I sat down as my parents stood beside Sunshine. Eyes filled with tears, Daddy spoke, "Sunshine, you reminded me of an American soldier. You faced an enemy that wanted to kill, steal, and destroy your life, and you fought your battle with great courage. As a World War II Bronze Star recipient, I would like to present you with a medal of honor."

Daddy pinned the golden sunflower medal on Sunshine. Momma unrolled a scroll and proclaimed:

"Today, July 22, 1961, *we salute our hero*, LeAnne Taylor, Miss Sunshine, on her brave acts of courage. The Friend Family presents Sunshine with a Gold Star Medal. Sunshine has smiled in the midst of hurt, she's laughed in the midst of heartache, and she's loved in the midst of pain.
Sunshine is and forever will be a hero in our book.

According to Noah,

sun·shine / sən "shin / *noun*
2 : something (as a person, condition, or influence) that radiates warmth, cheer, or happiness

Sunshine, thanks for shining your light!

*Your Friends Forever,
The Friend Family*"

The rainbows disappeared, the sun set, and the sunflowers bowed their heads. It was after midnight when we returned home. We had so much to be thankful for. We skipped our bedtime stories and said our nighttime prayers. Tonight all the Friends had sweet dreams.

THE END

The next mornin', I woke up to a huge commotion takin' place in the kitchen. I thought I heard Momma shoutin', "Boys, were you born in a barn? Please close the door! Do you want birds flying in?" Then I heard a flappin' noise, some doors slammin', Momma screamin', "Look out! Oh, no! I can't . . ."

To find out what happens you'll have to read the next book!

Keep your eyes peeled
and look for the sunflowers!
Every full illustration in this book
has a sunflower hidden in the page.

Happy hunting!

Sgt. Harold Eugene Friend
"My Daddy –
An American Hero"

Jean Vivian Friend
"The Friends' Private
Nurse"

The Friend Wedding
"Daddy & Momma – Goo-Goo Eyes"

Friendly Acres Farm
"Walkin' in the Cornfield"

Momma & Grandma
Brombaugh
"Hats again!"

Ronald, Ronda, & Duane
"Our New Black & White
Television"

Harold Friend – Summer of 2005
"1850 Farmhouse"

Friends' Fireplace
"Santa's Entrance"

LeAnne Taylor
"A Farmer's Daughter, too!"

The Friends
"Practicin' the Piano in
the Parlor"

Ray Schlee
"Daddy's Tank Gunner"

Hats off to Heroes! Grandma Stella Friend
"The Friend Cousins"

Rainbow of Love

words and music by R. Friend

HEADQUARTERS 13TH ARMORED DIVISION
SPO 263   U. S. ARMY

CITATION

For Award of The Bronze Star Medal

HAROLD E. FRIEND, 25 614 650, Sergeant, Armored, Company "D," 24th Tank Battalion, for heroic achievement in connection with military operations against an enemy of the United States on 1 May 1945, near Eggenfelden, Germany. When another vehicle was struck by bazooka fire, Sergeant Friend, tank commander, completely disregarded his personal safety by leaving his tank and rushing to the aid of two men and an officer. Making his way for 50 yards under an intense barrage of hostile fire, he succeeded in evacuating the casualties to the safety of a ditch. He then administered first aid so efficiently that the Medical Aid Men had merely to place the wounded men in their ambulance when they arrived. Sergeant Friend's instructions to his crew before leaving the tank were so explicit that the crew played an important role in operations. Sergeant Friend's great courage and devotion to duty are worthy of the high traditions of the Army. Entered military service from Alexandria, Ohio.

JOHN MILLIKIN
Major General, U.S. Army
Commanding

Check Out Our Kids Websites

www.DownOnFriendlyAcres.com

What's fact and what's fiction in "R. Friend – Down On Friendly Acres?" Did Diane really disappear? Was the farmhouse really built in 1850 with a dumbwaiter? Did Duane and Ronda really throw things down the laundry chute? Did Mr. Friend keep a journal during WORLD WAR II? Did he really give a doll to his gunner?

Songs! Games! Pictures! Contests!

Enter the "Friend of R. Friend's Author Contest!"
Enter the "Funniest Farmer's Tale."
Email your clothespin picture.
* And much more!

Check out our Educators and Parents Website

www.SunflowerSeedsPress.com

Order the "Down On Friendly Acres" series through our websites!
"R. Friend – Swallows Her Pride" #1 (forgiveness)
"R. Friend – Time Out At Home" #2 (patience)
"R. Friend – Hats Off To Heroes" #3 (kindness)

Coming in Spring of 2006
"R. Friend – Panic In The Pig Pen!" #4 (perseverance)

"What Do Friends of R. Friend Say?"
Children and parents are saying . . .

"My son, Stephen, finished the books, *Swallows Her Pride* and *Time Out at Home*. He loved reading your books. Stephen said, 'I learned something . . . these books help you be a better person. I like it when I learn stuff like this and she makes it so funny. Can we get the rest of the books?'"
Pam & Stephen – Lebanon, Ohio

"My two daughters, Molli and Abbie, are second and fifth graders respectively...they thought you were 'the best author that had ever visited our school.' I have to agree . . . your presentation was wonderful."
Krista (Teacher & Parent),
Mollie, & Abbie – Springboro, Ohio

"IT WAS THE BEST BOOK I HAVE EVER READ AND THAT IS THE TRUTH!!!!! I CAN'T WAIT TO GET MY HANDS ON THE NEXT BOOK!!!"
Ashley – Cookeville, Tennessee

Educators are saying . . .

"Ronda Friend became 'our friend' the minute she walked through the doors of our school. Ronda's books are silly but heartwarming family stories that students will not forget. Students still ask for Ronda's books and remember the catchy phrases." *Pat Messner, Media Specialist – Lebanon, Ohio*

". . . An exceptionally gifted storyteller! Adults and children alike find her performances entertaining, enlightening, and engaging!"
Judy Thompson, former Fields Service Manager for Scholastic Book Fairs and bookstore owner – Washington, Georgia

Remember...
Grandma Brombaugh says,

"*Presents* put a smile on a face for a day, but
kind words bring love, joy, and hope
to the heart forever!!!"

About the Author

Photo: Bob Fitzpenn

Ronda Friend (R. Friend) is a child at heart who has worked with children for over thirty years. As a professional story-teller, she has captivated hundreds of thousands of children with her music, animation, and big heart. Administrators, teachers, parents, and children describe her presentations as *"heart-warming, energizing, laughter to tears and back again, fun, sensitive, caring, entertaining, and refreshing."* As author of the "Down on Friendly Acres" series, her vision is to plant seeds of a different kind – seeds of kindness, patience, laughter, perseverance, and honesty into the lives of children and their families.

She holds a B.A. degree in education with a minor in music. Ronda has two grown children, Jeremy and Stephanie, and lives with her husband, Bill, in Franklin, Tennessee.

Check out www.SunflowerSeedsPress.com for booking information